Gossie

Olivier Dunrea

WALKER BOOKS
AND SUBSIDIARIES

LONDON · BOSTON · SYDNEY · AUCKLAND

For Ed

First published in Great Britain 2004 by Walker Books Ltd
87 Vauxhall Walk, London SE11 5HJ

This edition published 2006

2 4 6 8 10 9 7 5 3 1

© 2002 Olivier Dunrea
Published by arrangement with Houghton Mifflin Company

This book has been typeset in Shannon

Printed in China

British Library Cataloguing in Publication Data:
a catalogue record for this book is available from the British Library

ISBN-13: 978-1-4063-0118-2
ISBN-10: 1-4063-0118-3

www.walkerbooks.co.uk

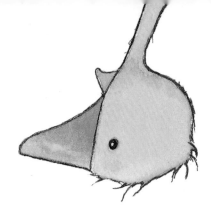

This is Gossie.
Gossie is a gosling.

A small, yellow gosling who
likes to wear bright red boots.

Every day.

She wears them
when she eats.

She wears them
when she sleeps.

She wears them when she rides.

She wears them when she hides.

But what Gossie *really* loves
is to wear her bright red boots
when she goes for walks.

Every day.

She walks backwards.

She walks forwards.

She walks uphill.

She walks downhill.

She walks in the rain.

She walks in the snow.

Gossie loves to wear
her bright red boots!

Every day.

One morning Gossie could
not find her bright red boots.

She looked everywhere.
Under the bed.

Over the wall.

In the barn.

Under the hens.

Gossie looked and looked
for her bright red boots.

They were gone.
Gossie was heartbroken.

Then she saw them.

They were walking.

On someone else's feet!

"Great boots!" said Gertie.
Gossie smiled.

Almost every day.

Gossie is a gosling.
A small, yellow gosling who
likes to wear bright red boots.